SWAMP
CURRITUCK SOUND
ATLAN
OCEA

ATHENEUM BOOKS FOR YOUNG READERS
An imprint of Simon & Schuster Children's Publishing Division
1230 Avenue of the Americas, New York, New York 10020

For information about special discounts for bulk purchases, please contact Simon & Schuster Special Sales at 1-866-506-1949 or business@simonandschuster.com.
The Simon & Schuster Speakers Bureau can bring authors to your live event. For more information or to book an event, contact the Simon & Schuster Speakers Bureau at 1-866-248-3049 or visit our website at www.simonspeakers.com.
Book design by Debra Sfetsios
The text for this book is set in Adobe Caslon.
The illustrations for this book are rendered in gouache and ink.
Manufactured in China
0210 WGL
First Edition
10 9 8 7 6 5 4 3 2 1
Library of Congress Cataloging-in-Publication Data
Griffin, Kitty.
The ride : the legend of Betsy Dowdy / Kitty Griffin ; illustrated by Marjorie Priceman. – 1st ed.
p. cm.
Summary: Recounts the legend of North Carolina teenager Betsy Dowdy, whose courageous ride on a cold December night in 1775 may have played a crucial role in the American Revolution.
ISBN 978-1-4169-2816-4 (hardcover)
1. United States–History–Revolution, 1775–1783–Juvenile fiction. 2. North Carolina–History–Revolution, 1775–1783–Juvenile fiction. [1. United States–History–Revolution, 1775–1783–Fiction. 2. North Carolina–History–Revolution, 1775–1783–Fiction. 3. Horsemanship–Fiction.] I. Priceman, Marjorie, ill. II. Title.
PZ7.G881358Ri 2010 [E]–dc22 2009020841

To my darling daughters, Danika and Beatrice, for making this journey so joyful.

To Emma, for being a steady light on a road which sometimes grew dark. —K. G.

DON'T TREAD ON ME

by Kitty Griffin
Illustrated by Marjorie Priceman

ATHENEUM BOOKS FOR YOUNG READERS
New York London Toronto Sydney

Sometimes legends start in the quietest of places.

On December 8, 1775, a legend began on the barrier island of Currituck, North Carolina.

Like the residents in the rest of the American colonies, the people of North Carolina wanted freedom from England's rule. King George III answered them with punishing laws and soldiers to enforce them.

When sixteen-year-old Betsy Dowdy heard Papa talk about war approaching, she felt as helpless as a ghost crab skittering along the sand.

She couldn't stop King George. She couldn't fight as a soldier.

With her pony Bess standing as close as a shadow, Betsy stared out at the choppy waters of the Currituck Sound. Bess sniffed Betsy's apron pocket. Betsy reached in and pulled out an apple. One thing she could do was take care of the ponies she loved.

Just then she saw a boat bobbing in the water. Papa came running.

"It's late," he said. "Something's wrong."

Sam Jarvis started shouting before he reached the dock. "Lord Dunmore and the redcoats are marching to Great Bridge. They're after your ponies and our supplies."

"We have to stop them!" Betsy cried.

"Only General Skinner's militia can, but his camp is fifty miles away," Mr. Jarvis said.

Papa shook his head. “There’s not a man who could get word to the general tonight. The ride is too long and too dangerous.”

Betsy watched them leave to warn their neighbors. Warning folks wasn't enough. The redcoats had to be stopped.

No one was going to take away all she loved.

She knew Bess could outrun any horse. They could make the ride.

Betsy stuffed her wool cloak and dry socks into an oiled leather bag. She slid her knife into its sheath. From the cupboard, she took her warmest linsey-woolsey shirt. She tightened the stays on her vest and pulled on her leather breeches.

Her hand shook as she wrote "Skinner" on her slate for Papa to see.

SKI

Betsy gave a loud whistle and Bess trotted up. "We need to be strong, Bess," she said, pulling herself up. "We're riding for freedom."

She guided Bess to the channel crossing. They paused at the water's edge. She couldn't stop King George. She couldn't fight as a soldier. But she could ride.

"Go on, girl," she said.

With a splash, Bess plunged in. Betsy gasped as cold water swirled around her. The flow lifted her off her pony's back, but she gripped Bess's mane until they reached shore.

The night air stiffened Betsy's fingers as she pulled the dry socks up over her legs. She fastened her cloak tightly, but nothing stopped her chattering teeth.

They followed the narrow path through the marshland into the forest. Bess snorted and stood still. Her ears flicked. Through the trees Betsy saw moonlight reflect off a pair of staring eyes. She gripped the hilt of her knife. Was it a bear?

She pressed her heels into Bess's flanks, silently urging the pony on.

When the path led to the hard-packed dirt road, Betsy leaned forward and whispered, “Now, Bess, run.” Away the pony flew.

Betsy held on. She prayed for their way to be safe from outlaws. She prayed Bess wouldn’t stumble. The miles fell behind them as Bess kept a steady pace. Surely they were near Lamb’s Ferry.

As they rounded a bend, a barking pack of dogs leapt at them. Bess reared. Betsy tumbled off.

"Who goes there?" demanded a booming voice.

"Betsy Dowdy from Currituck," she replied, her voice trembling.

It was Mr. Lamb.

Betsy sat up. "Dunmore has soldiers marching to Great Bridge. I have to warn General Skinner. Take us across the river."

"Are you wearing breeches, girl?" Mr. Lamb held out his hand and pulled her up.

"I would have drowned in skirts," she answered. "Mr. Lamb, if I don't give warning, the British will take everything from us. Bess and I have made it this far. You have to take us across. You *have* to."

"You're a pepper pot, Betsy Dowdy. Come on." He helped get Bess onto the flat-bottomed boat.

As he poled them over, Mr. Lamb gave Betsy advice. "Keep to the road. Past Hertford are the Perquimans Highlands. There, head south. The second river is Yeopim. Ah, Betsy, God keep you safe. Liberty is our dream."

"Liberty."

Betsy repeated the word as Bess's hooves pounded the dirt.

"Liberty."

She said it out loud, letting the word comfort her.

Bess jumped to clear something. Betsy glanced back and saw a snarling fox guarding its kill.

The path seemed to change. Had they reached the Highlands? How many more miles?

Betsy's eyes began to close.

If only she could sleep, just a little bit . . .

A low tree bough slapped her hard in the face. Betsy was flung to the ground. She wiped dirt from her mouth. Another fall. She couldn't do this. It was too far, too much.

But if she gave up, Papa could go to prison for his angry words against King George. She would lose her home. The colonies might never be free.

Bess whinnied. She pawed the ground by Betsy.

“You’re right, girl. Everything depends on us.” Betsy rose to her feet and mounted her pony.

She couldn't stop the king. She couldn't fight as a soldier. But she could ride.

Finally the pale gray light of morning pushed away the darkness. Betsy yawned and slowed Bess down to an easy lope.

"Halt," called a young soldier on the road.

"Is this General Skinner's camp?" Betsy asked.

He stared. "Who are you?"

She pushed back the hood of her cloak so he could see her face. "Betsy Dowdy. I've got news for the general."

"The general is up there." The soldier pointed.

Betsy pressed her heels into her pony once more. "We've done it, Bess."

After listening to her story, the general said, “I’ll take my men and we’ll give Dunmore a fight. Great Bridge is too important to yield to the redcoats.”

“My pony needs to be cared for,” Betsy said.

“Aye, both of you do,” the general said. “I suggest you eat and rest. Miss Betsy, North Carolina is in your debt. You are a remarkable young woman.”

"No, sir," Betsy answered.
"I just know how to ride."

Author's Note

As Betsy rode back to Currituck Sound, the men of North Carolina marched to Great Bridge. They met up with the Virginia militia, and together the soldiers fought the British troops.

The victory ultimately won by the colonial soldiers on December 9, 1775, was critical because it proved that the mighty British army could be defeated.

On July 4, 1776, just seven months after Betsy's ride, the American colonies united and declared independence.

It cannot be proved that Betsy Dowdy really existed, but her legend lives on. In Elizabeth City, North Carolina, the Daughters of the American Revolution named their chapter after Betsy Dowdy because her name represents the spirit of freedom—the spirit that created a nation.